COYOTE RAID
IN CACTUS CANYON

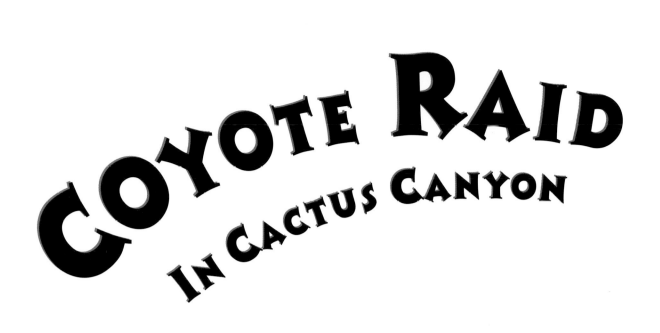

BY JIM ARNOSKY

G. P. Putnam's Sons / New York

Published simultaneously in Canada. Manufactured in China by South China Printing Co. Ltd.
Designed by Gunta Alexander. Text set in Catull.
The art was done in watercolor.

Library of Congress Cataloging-in-Publication Data
Arnosky, Jim. Coyote raid in Cactus Canyon / by Jim Arnosky.   p. cm.
Summary: Four young coyotes harass the animals in a desert canyon until they run into a rattlesnake.
[1. Desert animals–Fiction. 2. Deserts–Fiction. 3. Coyote–Fiction. 4. Rattlesnakes–Fiction. 5. Snakes–Fiction.]
I. Title. PZ7.A7384Co 2005 [E]–dc22 2003021950 ISBN 0-399-23413-6
3 5 7 9 10 8 6 4 2

FOR CONNER

It was a hot and windless desert day.
On the canyon slopes, cactus stood
tall against a blue sky. High up
in the arms of the tallest cactus,
a wren was busy making her nest.

Down on the stone-covered ground, a cottontail hopped softly. Quail moved noiselessly behind green and purple prickly pears.

An antelope squirrel perched on top of a cactus log to nibble a fallen desert flower. All was peaceful in the canyon. But the mood was about to change.

The coyote gang was coming
and they were bringing trouble.

Ornery and full of mischief, four young
coyotes headed down the rocky slope
to the canyon floor.

They sniffed out the cottontail and
chased him into a thorny thicket.
They barked at the cactus wren
until she flew from her nest.

The coyotes flushed the quail from
their cover behind the prickly pears.
Then they stuck their snouts into
the cactus log to growl at the
antelope squirrel hiding inside.

When they could not find any other animals
to chase or frighten, the coyotes turned
and faced each other.

Slowly the four young coyotes circled,
watching one another's every move.

The wren flew to the top of a prickly pear
to see the coyote standoff. The cottontail and
squirrel peeked out from their hiding places.

And the quail gathered close together to watch as one.

Suddenly the coyotes rushed one another and began to brawl, snarling and snapping their jaws. They tumbled right on top of a rattlesnake slithering by.

The startled snake quickly coiled
and rattled. The coyotes froze,
their eyes fixed on the huge snake.
She was ready to strike.

The four coyotes backed away
until they felt safe and brave again.
Then they growled and barked and
showed the snake their own sharp fangs.
But the snake held her ground and
struck out at the coyote gang.

The four coyotes turned and ran,
disappearing over the canyon rim.
The rattlesnake slithered on her way.

The quail settled back down.
The cottontail hopped quietly.
The antelope squirrel found
another fallen cactus flower
to nibble.

And the wren flew back to
the arms of the tallest cactus,
carrying a fuzzy clump of
coyote fur for her nest.

The canyon was
a peaceful place
again.